Date: 11/8/21

ADDERALL
AFFECTING LIVES

BY MARTHA LONDON

MOMENTUM

Published by The Child's World®
1980 Lookout Drive • Mankato, MN 56003-1705
800-599-READ • www.childsworld.com

ISBN 9781503844889 (Reinforced Library Binding)
ISBN 9781503846371 (Portable Document Format)
ISBN 9781503847569 (Online Multi-user eBook)
LCCN 2019957686

Printed in the United States of America

Some names and details have been changed
throughout this book to protect privacy.

CONTENTS

MOMENTUM

FAST FACTS

What It Is

► Adderall is a **prescription** drug. It is a **stimulant**. It helps people focus and gives them more energy.

► Doctors prescribe Adderall to people with attention deficit hyperactivity disorder (ADHD). It helps them control impulses and pay attention.

How It's Used

► Adderall is prescribed as a pill.

► Some people who **abuse** Adderall crush up the pills and snort the powder. Other people inject Adderall. These methods increase the risk of **overdose**.

Physical Effects

► Adderall abuse can lead to trouble sleeping, loss of appetite, and loss of strength.

► Adderall abuse can cause dizziness. It may also cause increased heart rate and body temperature.

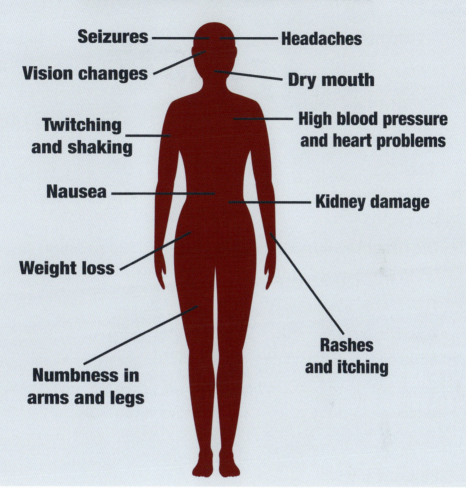

Side Effects of Adderall Abuse

Seizures

Headaches

Vision changes

Dry mouth

Twitching and shaking

High blood pressure and heart problems

Nausea

Kidney damage

Weight loss

Numbness in arms and legs

Rashes and itching

Mental Effects

► People who take Adderall experience feelings of happiness and confidence.

► **Withdrawal** from Adderall can cause irritability, anxiety, and depression.

► People who abuse Adderall may become **addicted**. They may need professional help to quit.

CHAPTER ONE

EXTRA HELP

Crickets chirped as Dylan walked back to his house from his shift at the grocery store. It was past 11 o'clock at night, and Dylan still had homework to do when he got home. He had to work hard to get good grades in his college classes. But Dylan was exhausted.

His keys jingled as he unlocked the door. Some of his roommates were playing video games in the living room. The sound of crashing vehicles and screeching tires on the screen filtered through the house.

Dylan went to his room and closed the door. He threw his wallet and keys on his bed. His lamp shined on his thick chemistry textbook. Dylan's eyelids were heavy. He was never going to get his homework done without help.

◄ **Some students misuse Adderall to help them focus on homework.**

▲ **Doctors will check for signs of ADHD and may run tests before prescribing Adderall.**

Dylan pulled open his top desk drawer. A bottle of pills sat at the bottom. He had filled the prescription a week ago. But he had not taken any of the pills yet. Dylan had gone to a doctor. He had lied and convinced the doctor that he had ADHD. He had said that he needed Adderall to help him focus on his homework. When Dylan mentioned how Adderall worked for his friends with ADHD, the doctor had raised her eyebrows. She had said that Adderall was a powerful drug. It could be addicting. Dylan had assured the doctor he just needed a little extra help focusing. The doctor ran some tests and then gave Dylan a prescription.

The bottle's label read, "Take one tablet twice daily." Each tablet, or pill, was 10 milligrams. Dylan twisted the cap off and took one pill from the bottle. He drank some water and got to work.

Four hours later, Dylan was still wide awake. The Adderall was working. He could not sleep if he wanted to. He had finished his homework, but he could not stop working. So Dylan also cleaned his room and organized his desk. He even sorted his papers.

At five o'clock in the morning, Dylan finally fell into his bed. He woke up three hours later in time to get ready for his 9 a.m. class. Three hours was not enough sleep. Dylan was tired.

YOUTH AND ADDERALL

As of 2016, approximately 6.1 million kids in the United States were diagnosed with ADHD. Some are prescribed Adderall. Adderall helps kids with ADHD concentrate. But many people who do not have ADHD also take Adderall. They use it without a prescription. One study in 2015 showed that one in six college students misuses stimulants such as Adderall. Many of them buy pills from other students who have a prescription.

He swallowed one more Adderall pill so that he would stay awake in class.

For the first couple of weeks, Dylan felt great. He had so much energy when he first started taking Adderall. But the medication was not helping him as much as it used to. Dylan was not taking 10 milligrams anymore. He started taking more pills to get the same effects. Now he was taking up to 100 milligrams every day. He had to take Adderall to get out of bed on the weekends. His hands shook, and his heart pounded when he took the drug. Dylan felt his pulse in his ears. The Adderall was also affecting his blood flow. His toes and hands were always cold.

When Dylan tried to stop taking Adderall, all he wanted to do was sleep. His body crashed. He needed a lot of sleep. Sometimes, he slept through all of his morning classes. When Dylan did not take Adderall, he got angry easily. Dylan yelled at his friends for little things. His friends stopped hanging out with him. Dylan knew that Adderall was negatively affecting him. But he was afraid to quit. He did not know how he would get all of his schoolwork done without it. Dylan knew he needed help. He made an appointment with his doctor. He would do what it would take to overcome his addiction. He was ready to be back to his old self.

People may sleep more when the Adderall ▶ wears off. But the sleep may not be restful.

CHAPTER TWO

A HEAVY PRICE

Sweat dripped down Sara's nose. She looked down at the treadmill display. Her heart rate was up, and she had just finished her 45-minute jog. TVs spanned the walls. Some showed a soccer game. Others showed scrolling inspirational quotes. Sara laid a mat on the floor and stretched. As she finished her cooldown, she felt great.

Sara was working hard to lose 10 pounds (4.5 kg) for her wedding. She went to the gym four days a week. She ate a balanced diet. She had even seen a doctor a few weeks ago. Sara felt like she was doing everything right.

Sara headed to the locker room. Her towel hung over her shoulder. Before she went to shower, she stepped on the scale. Sara was sure she had lost a few pounds. But when she looked at the scale, she saw that she had not lost any weight.

◄ **People may abuse Adderall to help them achieve short-term goals such as weight loss.**

▲ It is illegal to take Adderall without a doctor's prescription.

This was the sixth week in a row. Sara knew that losing weight took time, but she was sure that by now she should have seen some results. She sighed and headed to the showers, disappointed.

A few days later, Sara was hanging out with her friend Matt. They each had a big salad and a glass of water. She told him how frustrated she was about not losing any weight. He listened closely and nodded. Matt put his fork down to speak.

Matt told her that when he first started taking Adderall, he lost some weight. He explained it was a side effect for some people.

He was not as hungry when he took it. He used the Adderall to treat his ADHD, but he did not need as many pills as the doctor gave him. He offered Sara some of his Adderall pills. Sara thought about it. She really wanted to lose some weight before her wedding. She agreed to Matt's offer.

The next day, Sara's doorbell rang. Matt stood outside and handed her a little bag of pills. She gave him some cash. He told her he could get her more pills if she needed them.

Sara decided to take one pill each day before she went to the gym. The first day, she spent twice as much time at the gym as she usually did. She had so much energy. Sara liked how she was able to push herself at the gym. That evening, instead of making a big dinner, she had a small salad. She was also able to get all of the things on her to-do list done.

After the first week, Sara had lost 3 pounds (1.4 kg). Finally, she was losing weight. She asked Matt for just one more bag. Sara told herself that once she had a routine, she would not need the pills anymore.

But after a month of buying more and more pills from Matt, Sara had to admit that something was wrong. None of her clothes fit anymore. They all hung loosely off her body. Even the new clothes she bought a month ago were too big. Some people at work started asking if she was sick. Sara felt shaky all the time.

She knew that taking Adderall and over-exercising was hurting her. She was having a hard time sleeping. At work she felt dizzy. Sometimes she felt nauseated.

One evening, while sitting at the kitchen table, Sara leaned her head on her fist. She pushed her food around her plate. She was not hungry, but she wanted to eat. Sara had to tell someone about her addiction. She called her friend, Lyla. Lyla was supportive. She promised to take Sara to a **detox** center the next day. She said that detox centers help people slowly stop their use of Adderall. Doctors are at the centers. They are there to make sure patients are healthy as they quit Adderall. Then, Sara could get into a **rehabilitation** (rehab) center and get help for her Adderall addiction.

FINDING HELP

Some patients stay at rehab centers full-time. Patients typically stay there for up to three months. After rehab, some doctors recommend that patients have individual or group therapy. Therapy will help keep them from abusing the drug again.

CHAPTER THREE

TALKING ABOUT IT

Sunlight streamed through the window. Owen looked at the clock next to him. It was 8 a.m. He could hear his partner, Kelly, in the kitchen. Owen wondered how long she had been awake.

Kelly bustled around. All the cabinets were cleared out. The coffeemaker bubbled on the counter. Owen asked how long Kelly had been up. She said she had a tough time sleeping again. She had gotten up at 4 a.m. Owen asked if she wanted to sit down and have some coffee with him. Kelly spoke quickly. She said that she was on a roll and wanted to finish organizing the kitchen.

Owen looked at Kelly. Her pupils were big, black saucers. She was **high** again. Owen knew she was addicted to Adderall. But he did not know how to bring it up to her. Kelly did not think she had a problem.

◄ **Overworking is a sign of Adderall abuse.**

In the early afternoon, Owen knew Kelly's pills were wearing off. She was acting differently. He asked if she wanted to go with him to walk the dog. Kelly snapped at him. She said she had too much to do around the house. Owen clipped the leash to the dog's collar and walked out the door.

He did not feel like he could talk to Kelly about anything. Her mood swings were huge from when she took Adderall to when the drug started to wear off. Kelly could be talking quickly one moment and yelling the next. Owen did not like when Kelly was using Adderall. Recently, she had been taking a lot of it.

When Owen got back, Kelly was sitting in the living room. He asked if she had finished her tasks. She said she had. Owen asked Kelly if they could talk about her Adderall use.

Kelly did not seem like she wanted to. She crossed her arms, but she nodded. Owen sat down next to her on the couch. He told Kelly she was not acting like herself. She used to be so upbeat and positive. But now it was hard to have a conversation with her. Kelly listened.

Owen asked how he could help. Kelly told him she needed Adderall. When she tried to stop taking it, she felt so angry at Owen. Even when he was not doing anything wrong.

Increased irritability and mood swings are ▶ common side effects of using Adderall.

Kelly's head would hurt, too. When the pills wore off, she was so tired that it was hard to go to work.

Owen asked if she would go to a rehab center. They could help her stop using Adderall. Kelly nodded. She said she was scared. Owen gave Kelly a big hug. He promised everything would be okay. He would be with her every step of the way.

◄ When the body is used to Adderall, it
struggles to function without the drug.

CHAPTER FOUR

FROM A DOCTOR

Dr. Becca Johnson flipped through her folder. Her next appointment was with a person who was worried he had an Adderall addiction. She knocked on the door to the exam room. Then, Dr. Johnson walked inside and saw her patient waiting. He was sitting in a chair next to the exam table. He bounced his leg up and down. Dr. Johnson could tell he had been biting his nails. Going to a doctor could make any person nervous. If her patient was also misusing Adderall, he might be feeling even more anxious.

Dr. Johnson sat in the chair next to him. She introduced herself. He shook her hand and greeted her. Dr. Johnson started by asking her patient a few questions. She listened to him. She wrote down some notes, including a list of his **symptoms**. He was exhausted when he was not taking Adderall.

◄ **Taking Adderall can increase feelings of anxiety and nervousness.**

He had trouble sleeping. And he would often get angry at people close to him.

Once Dr. Johnson had her notes, she asked to measure the patient's blood pressure. She wrapped a blood pressure cuff around his arm. This would help check how his heart was doing. The air hissed as it slowly released the pressure from the patient's arm. He had high blood pressure. His heart was working too hard. Dr. Johnson asked the patient if he had a history of high heart rate. He told her that his heart had been pounding faster than usual for a couple weeks now. He could not seem to catch his breath. He was also having chest pains. The patient said he had tried to quit Adderall. But when he suddenly stopped, he felt like he could not function. He felt slow, and thinking was difficult. He had nightmares. And he was constantly anxious. So he started taking the pills again.

Dr. Johnson told him that those symptoms were common in people who abuse Adderall. But people should not stop taking Adderall all at once. It could be dangerous. The withdrawal effects can cause people to become sick. It can also cause them to become very depressed and anxious.

The patient looked at Dr. Johnson. He asked if she had any recommendations. She recommended he go to a detox center.

Abusing Adderall can lead to heart problems, such as ▶ high blood pressure. It can even cause heart attacks.

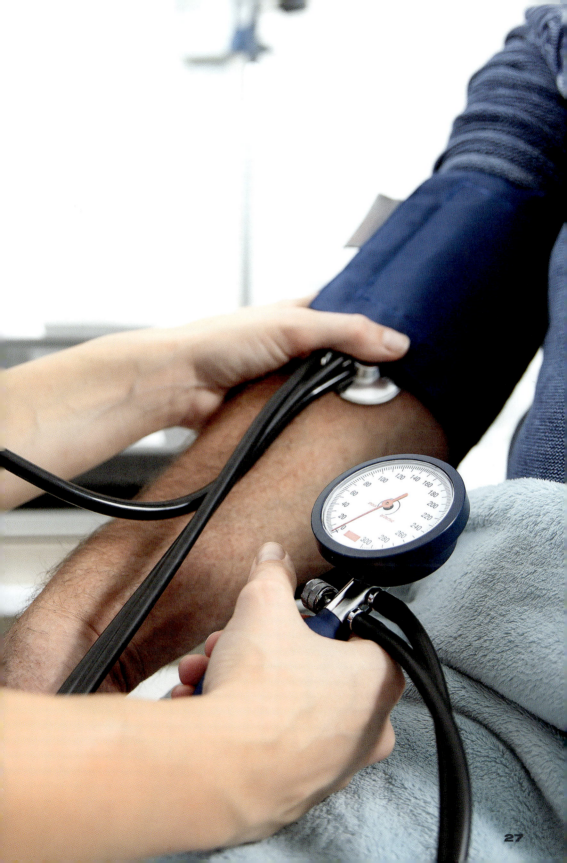

▲ People at rehab centers can help those
who struggle with drug addictions.

The people at the center would help him slowly stop using Adderall until he no longer needed it. Then Dr. Johnson walked him through the process of getting into a rehab center. She wrote down the names of three centers. Her pen scratched on the notepad. These centers could help her patient.

It is difficult for many people to admit they are struggling with an addiction. But there are resources out there to help people overcome their addiction to Adderall.

THINK ABOUT IT

► How would your life be different if you were addicted to Adderall?
► Do you think doctors should be careful when prescribing certain medicines to people? Explain your answer.
► Why do you think some highly addictive drugs such as Adderall are legal?

GLOSSARY

abuse (uh-BYOOZ): To abuse is to misuse a substance for nonmedical purposes. Those who abuse Adderall take it without a prescription.

addicted (uh-DIK-tid): Someone who is addicted feels a very strong need to do or have something regularly. People who use Adderall can become addicted to the drug.

detox (DEE-toks): A person who is going through a drug detox has stopped taking the drug and is feeling its effects. People going through drug detox can go to centers that will help them.

high (HY): Being high on a drug means having the feeling of euphoria from taking the drug. Kelly was high on Adderall.

overdose (OH-vur-dohss): An overdose is taking a dose of a drug that is too large and may either make people sick or kill them. Abusing Adderall can lead to an overdose.

prescription (pri-SKRIP-shuhn): A prescription is a doctor's written note that allows a patient to receive a given treatment. Adderall should only be taken with a prescription and if a person truly needs the drug.

rehabilitation (ree-uh-bil-uh-TAY-shun): Drug rehabilitation is a type of treatment for drug abuse. Rehabilitation centers help people with drug addictions quit using drugs.

stimulant (STIM-yuh-luhnt): A stimulant is a drug that excites the brain, increasing alertness and energy. Adderall is a stimulant.

symptoms (SIMP-tuhms): Symptoms show that a person has an illness or other physical problem. Dylan had withdrawal symptoms.

withdrawal (with-DRAW-uhl): Withdrawal is the experience of physical and mental effects when a person stops taking an addictive drug. People may need help going through withdrawal.

TO LEARN MORE

BOOKS

Alexander, Richard. *What's Drug Abuse?*
New York, NY: KidHaven Publishing, 2019.

Stanmyre, Jackie F. *Ritalin and Adderall.*
New York, NY: Cavendish Square, 2016.

Thiel, Kristin. *The Dangers of Prescription Drugs.*
New York, NY: PowerKids Press, 2020.

WEBSITES

Visit our website for links about addiction
to Adderall: **childsworld.com/links**

*Note to Parents, Teachers, and Librarians: We routinely verify our Web links to make
sure they are safe and active sites. So encourage your readers to check them out!*

SELECTED BIBLIOGRAPHY

Nall, Rachel. "Coping with an Adderall Crash." *Medical News Today*,
13 Apr. 2018, medicalnewstoday.com. Accessed 3 Dec. 2019.

"What Are the Side Effects of Adderall?" *American Addiction Centers*,
12 Sept. 2019, americanaddictioncenters.org. Accessed 3 Dec. 2019.

Williams, Sarah. "Adderall Addiction and Recovery Facts."
Recovery.org, 1 Nov. 2019, recovery.org. Accessed 3 Dec. 2019.

INDEX

ABOUT THE AUTHOR

Martha London lives in Minnesota. She is a writer and educator. Martha has written more than 100 books for young readers. When she isn't writing or teaching, you can find her hiking in the woods.